Night of the bedbugs

A
Silverline™
B O O K S
PRODUCTION

A DIVISION OF

Shadowline™ /**image**®

NIGHT OF THE BEDBUGS   ISBN: 978-1-60706-145-8   Ages 4-8

Published by Silverline Books a division of Shadowline, LLC/Image Comics, Inc. Office of publication: 2134 Allston Way, Second Floor, Berkeley, CA 94704. Copyright © 2010 PAUL FRICKE. All rights reserved. NIGHT OF THE BEDBUGS™ (including all prominent characters featured herein), its logo and all character likenesses are trademarks of PAUL FRICKE, unless otherwise noted. Image Comics ® and its logos are registered trademarks of Image Comics, Inc. Silverline Books and its logos are ™ and © 2010 Jim Valentino. All names, characters, events and locales in this publication are entirely fictional. Any resemblance to actual persons (living or dead), events or places, without satiric intent, is coincidental. No part of this publication may be reproduced or transmitted, in any form or by any means (except for short excerpts for review purposes) without the express written permission of Mr. Fricke.

PRINTED IN SOUTH KOREA   First Printing March, 2010

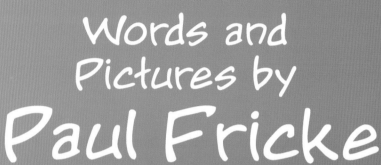

Words and
Pictures by
Paul Fricke

Edited by
Kristen Simon

Published by
Jim Valentino

With love
to my three girls,
Mary, Laura and Emily

...and thanks to
my family and friends
for their support
and encouragement.

She kissed my cheek, whispered,

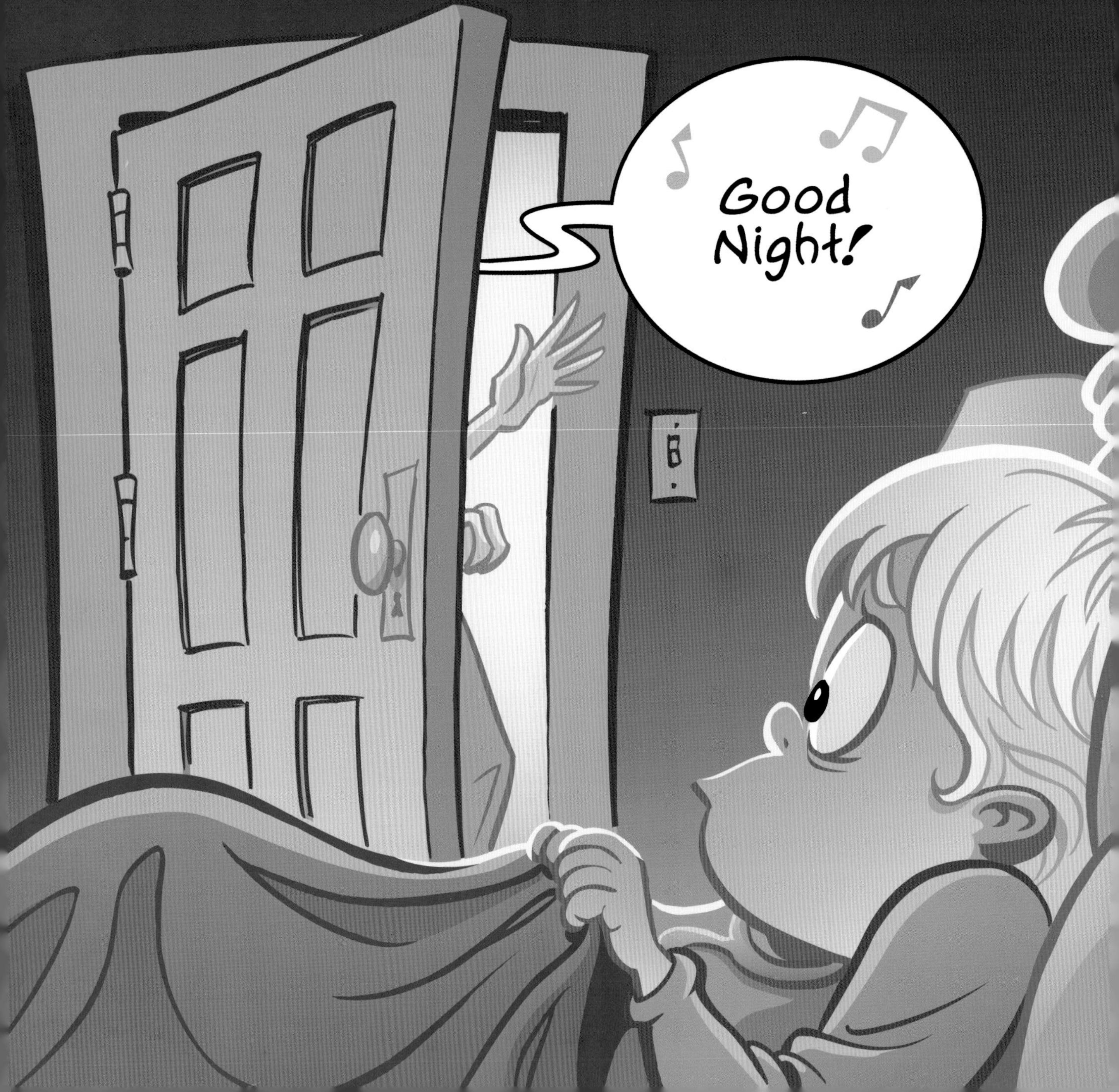

I lay there staring, open-eyed.
Gosh, it sure was dark outside!

The shadows played
upon my toys...

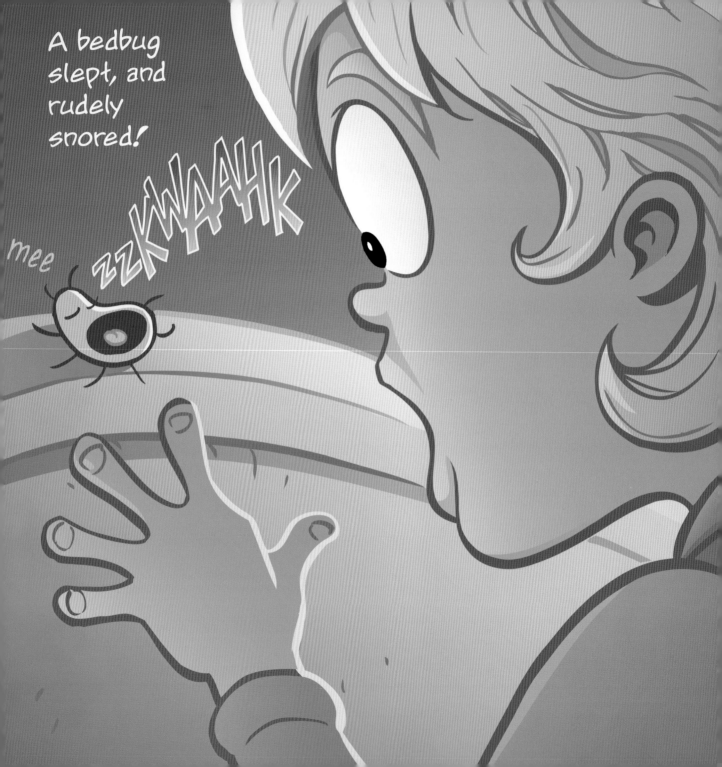

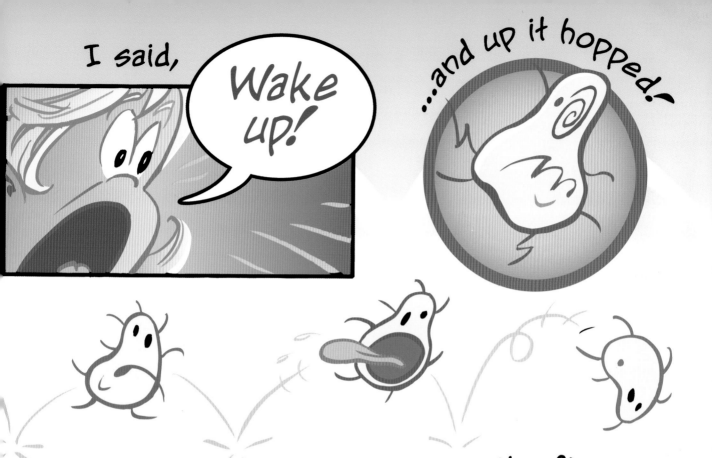

It bounced and skipped and flippity-flopped!

It jumped and twitched in tos-and-fros...

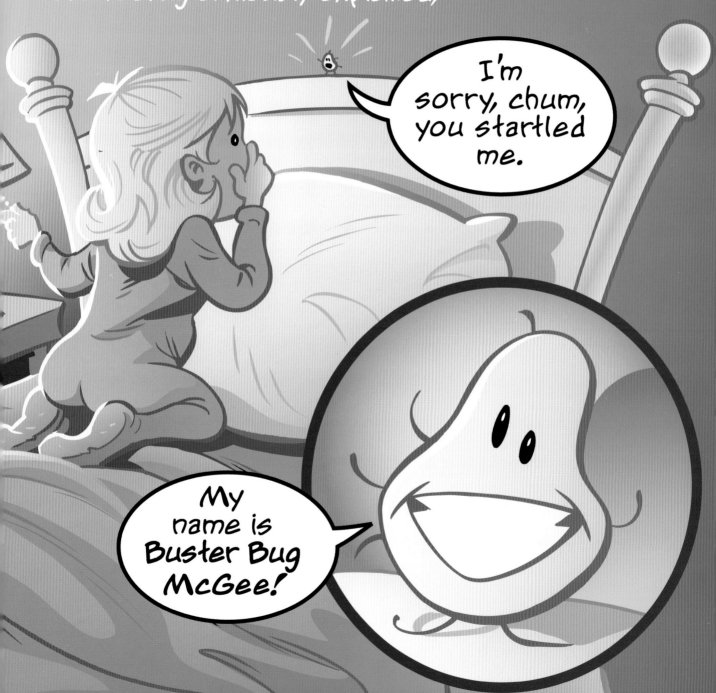

So I shook his hand ...

... or his leg, or his ... hair

They poured from the closet, from under the rug,

Bug after bug after bug after bug!

I met Barbara and Fred and Artie and Mac, All those names to remember – I couldn't keep track!

A slew of them sprung from my dresser drawer,

A frenzied fiesta of bugs crossed my floor!

Clearly, not one of them cared to be tardy, to a...

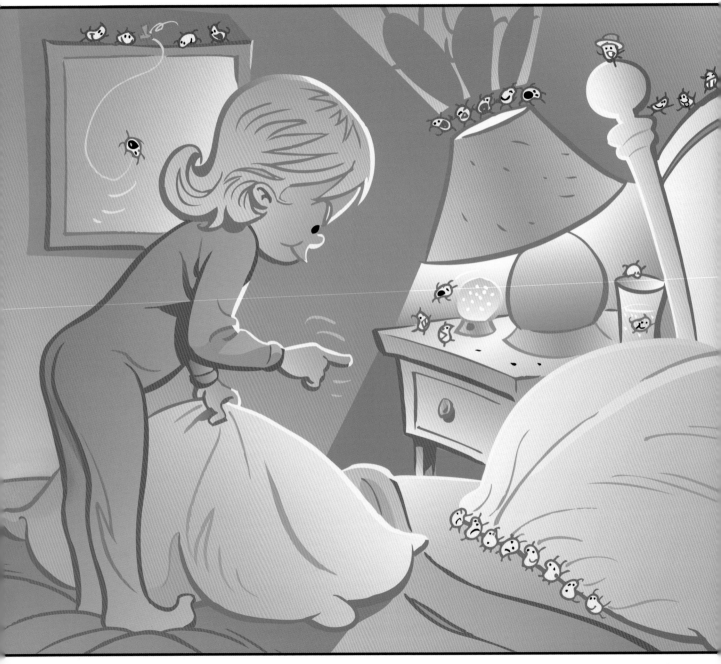

But they had to promise there would be no more biting

One circled the globe, a real globe-trotter...

A couple went swimming in my glass of water.

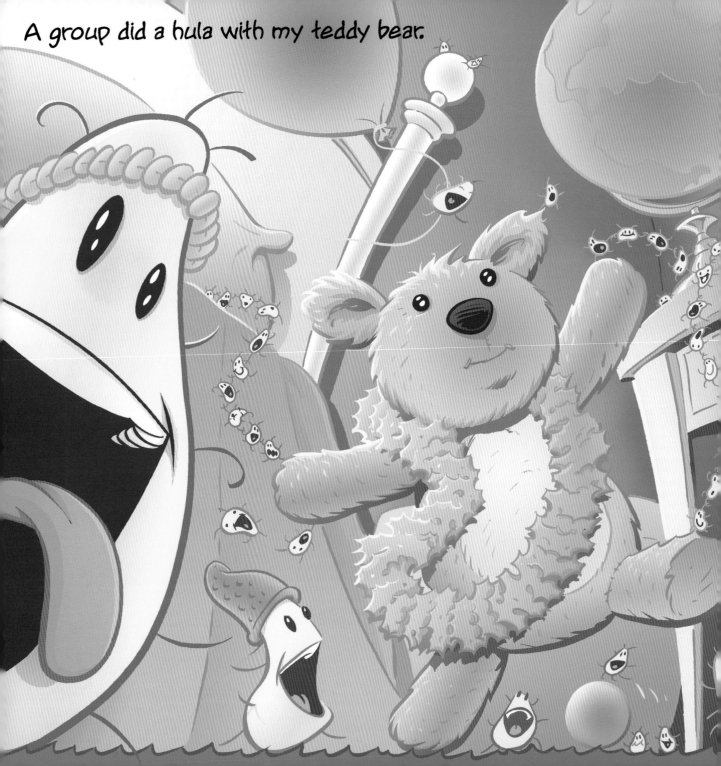
A group did a hula with my teddy bear.

My buddies were making a terrible riot,

So I had to tell them all to...

They offered their apologies,
and wished to make it up to me...

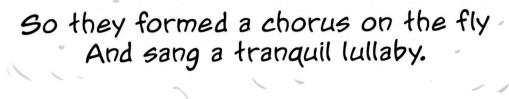
So they formed a chorus on the fly
And sang a tranquil lullaby.

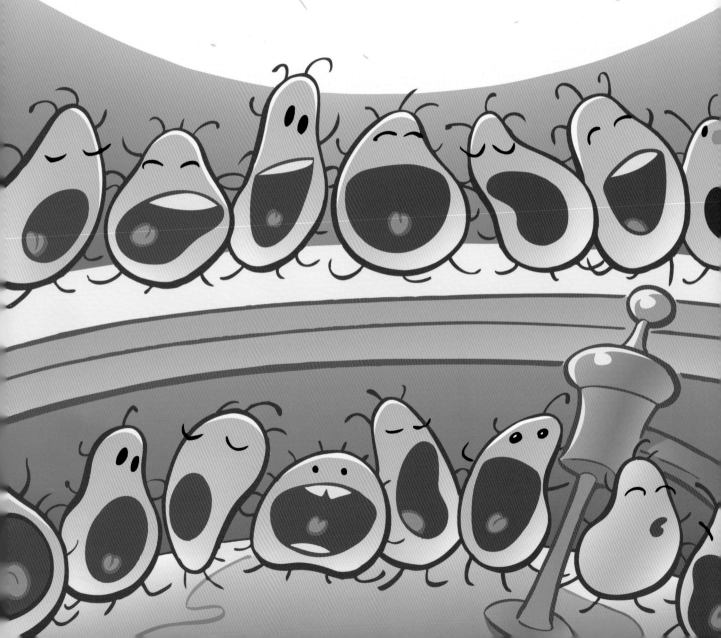

How gently my alarm was eased,
The most exquisite harmonies
Washed over me, into the night
A serenade by full moonlight.

Then each one hopped across the bed
Flitting sweet kisses on top of my head.

And when every last one
was tucked in, snug...

Then we drifted to sleep
in a Bedbug Group Hug.

Other fine  you and your family will enjoy...

T. RUNT! (4-8)
ISBN: 978-1-60706-074-1

DEAR DRACULA (Ages 4-8)
ISBN: 978-1-58240-970-2

PX! BOOK ONE: A GIRL AND HER PANDA
(YA) ISBN: 978-1-58240-820-0

PX! BOOK TWO: IN THE SERVICE OF
THE QUEEN (YA) ISBN: 978-1-58240-018-5

THE SURREAL ADVENTURES
OF EDGAR ALLAN POO (YA)
ISBN: 978-1-58240-816-3

THE SURREAL ADVENTURES
OF EDGAR ALLAN POO 2 (YA)
ISBN: 978-1-58240-975-7

EVIL & MALICE SAVE THE WORLD!
(9-12) ISBN: 978-1-60706-091-8

TIFFANY'S EPIPHANY (4-8) ISBN: 978-1-60706-110-6

MISSING THE BOAT (9-12)
ISBN: 978-1-60706-015-4

ROCKETBOTS
ISBN: 978-1-60706-167-0

BRUCE: THE LITTLE BLUE SPRUCE (4-8)
ISBN: 978-1-60706-008-6

Please visit our web-site for previews, character profiles, word searches, games, coloring pages and other fun stuff!

TIMOTHY AND THE TRANSGALACTIC
TOWEL (9-12)   ISBN: 978-1-60706-021-5

www.silverlinebooks.con

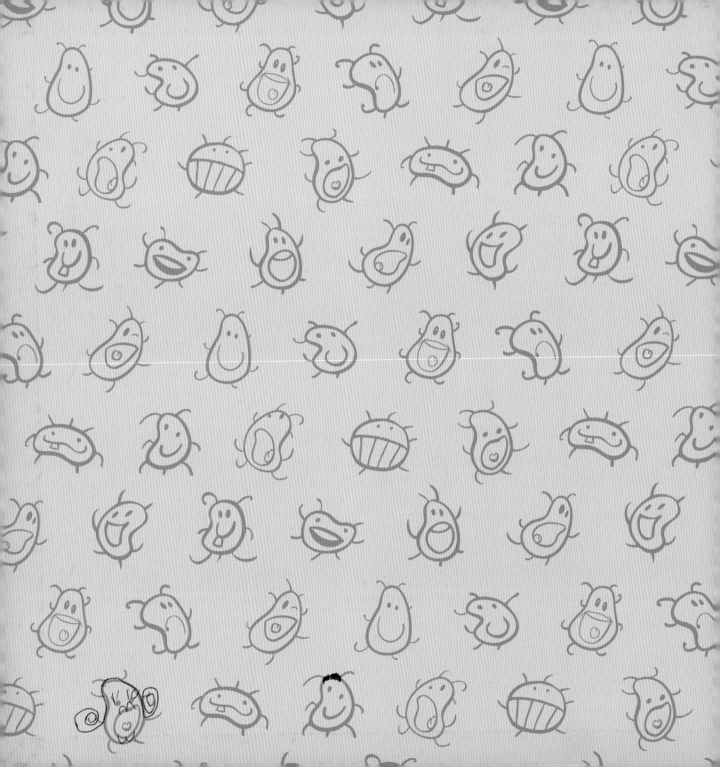